Bunny Strings

Amy Moore
Illustrations by Annette Cable

Harmony House Publishers
P. O. Box 90
Prospect, KY 40059
502-228-2010

©2008 by Amy Moore
Illustrations by Annette Cable

ISBN-13: 978-1-56469-206-1
Library of Congress Control Number: 2008926053

Design by Robinette Creative

Printed in China

To my children
who inspire me daily

Milly and Tate are five-year-old twins on their way to their first day of kindergarten. They cannot wait to find out all the exciting things they will learn.

As Milly and Tate settle into their new classroom, they meet their new teacher, Ms. Brown.

Ms. Brown announces to the class that their first project of the year will be to learn to tie shoes. Once all the children in the class learn, they will celebrate with an ice-cream party.

Milly and Tate were so excited about the ice-cream party, they began to practice as soon as they arrived home from school. It did not take long for both of them to realize that learning to tie shoes was much more difficult than it looked.

As days turned into weeks, most of the

class had learned to tie shoes, but not

Milly and Tate. Holding up an ice-cream

party for the whole class was not good.

That night before bed Milly and Tate

wished the very same wish at the very

same time. They wished they would each

learn to tie their shoes by the very next

day. Most people do not realize that

there are special fairies that grant wishes

that are made in pairs. The wish fairy

heard their wishes and left them a small

gift at the foot of their beds.

As the sun came up the next morning, Milly and Tate awoke to find something small and very interesting at the foot of their beds. The unusual shoe strings had a small note attached that read, *Bunny Strings.*

Inside the note read special instructions that explained how to use the *Bunny Strings.*

1 Take the end of the shoelaces, tie a knot and pull tight.

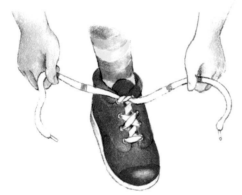

2 Make a loop by connecting #one with #two and hold tight.

3 Make another loop by connecting #three with #four and hold tight.

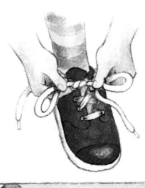

STRINGS

4   Connect all the black markings together by placing loop #three and #four on top of loop #one and #two. You will see a bunny head with two bunny ears.

5   Push the right bunny ear through the bunny head and pull tight.

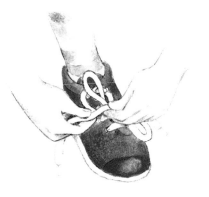

Milly and Tate each inserted the special

shoelaces into their sneakers and began

to practice. Within a very short period

of time the twins were tying shoes.

They could not wait to go to school

and show their teacher and classmates.

Mostly, they could not wait for

the ice-cream party.